Annemarie Nikolaus: Silenced

ANNEMARIE NIKOLAUS

SILENCED

"Nina, look, those are the colours of the Italian flag! Their pilots are the best." Manni helped his little sister to kneel up on the windowsill. "When I grow up, I'm going to be Italian!"

From the window in their high-rise building, they had a clear view of the air force base where the air show was taking place.

"They're coloring the sky!" Nina clapped her hands together enthusiastically. "It's so pretty. Mommy, come and look!"

Laura went over to her children, who were following the stunt pilots' maneuvers with beaming faces. "That's the *Frecce Tricolori* squadron."

A plane left the formation, spiraled upwards, turned and flew against the others in a wide loop. Suddenly, the sky exploded in a fireball that eclipsed the sun.

"Get down!" Laura dragged Nina off the windowsill.

Then the solo pilot collided with one of the oncoming fighter jets; shards of metal flew through the air. The windows rattled.

Laura pushed the children to the floor. Nina screamed.

In the next instant, both aircraft went up in flames. Burning, smoking wreckage plunged from the sky.

"Don't cry, darling." She wiped away Nina's tears mechanically with the sleeve of her jumper.

The windows were intact; slowly, Laura straightened up and peered over the ledge. Thick, black smoke was rising outside.

She rushed to the phone. "It's Laura Schreiner. Michael, a

stunt plane just exploded in mid-air. Clear a page – I'll be in the editorial office in an hour."

The children sat on the carpet. Manni swallowed hard and clutched his sister protectively.

Laura hesitated for a moment, but she had no choice. "You'll look after Nina, okay? Neither of you leaves the house! Mommy has to go to work for a bit."

Nina began to cry. "I'm scared."

Laura kneeled down next to her. "I'm going to get Mrs Breiner. And Daddy will be back soon." 'Hopefully', she thought, grabbing her camera equipment and rushing downstairs. 'Who knows what's going on out there?'

***

Acrid smoke drifted into Laura's face. Soon, she had to abandon her car. There was a stench of burning, and she had a coughing fit. Passing burning buildings and weaving between fire engines and ambulances, she reached the airfield. Soldiers had already sealed off a wide perimeter. She hung her press ID card around her neck.

"Stop, Ma'am." A military police officer blocked her way.

Laura pointed to her press ID. "Newspaper."

The officer shook his head. "No media, Ma'am. Military area."

The tail of an airplane protruded from the wreckage of a spectator stand. Several injured people lay on the ground opposite. The smoke brought tears to Laura's eyes. "I'm a journalist!"

"No media", the soldier insisted.

From the corner of her eye, she saw military police officers stopping a mobile medical unit, so she decided to give in, and moved towards the vehicle.

Before Laura reached it, the doctor and paramedics got out, but the soldiers wouldn't let them pass. The doctor protested loudly, swinging his medical kit, and tried to force his way past them. It was futile; they held him firmly.

Laura looked on for a moment in disbelief; then she looked back at the injured people on the airfield. The distance was only a hundred yards, and they wouldn't let the doctor go to them. She took a few steps back and began to take pictures.

Shortly afterwards, she sat at her desk in the office, hammering into the keys. "Military Police Blocks Rescue Efforts."

***

Laura's husband didn't get home until the next morning. "There were so many that were beyond our help. I was in the operating theater until just now."

Despite his exhaustion, Wilfried had remembered to bring the newspapers from the kiosk home with him. Laura stared at 'her' newspaper. "Catastrophe!" screamed the front page in large letters. "Crash involving three Italian stunt pilots." Below were pictures she had taken of the destruction to the affected district. But none of her photos from the air field, not a word about the military police hindering the work of the emergency services.

She flicked through all the pages twice, and then called her editor at home. "Michael, what did you do with my article? Why have you only used the news agencies' reports in the story?"

Michael cleared his throat, but said nothing.

"What's the matter? What's going on here?"

Finally, Michael answered. "We received a visit yesterday evening. So did all the newspapers around here. We've been asked for... confidentiality."

"Confidentiality?" Laura exploded. "What's confidential about an incident that caused dozens of deaths?"

Michael didn't answer directly. "It seems they'd like to avoid speculation about the cause of the crash."

"Who are 'they'? Who visited you yesterday?"

"There were two of them, in uniform. Secret service. They took your article with them." He sighed audibly.

"I see." A wave of heat rose through Laura's body. She stared at the telephone receiver with a deep frown before answering. "Well, that's interesting! I'll have to write a new one, then."

"Laura! What are you planning?"

"I'll help them to avoid speculation. Once learnt, never forgotten."

As Wilfried and the children ate breakfast, Laura left her coffee untouched and doodled pictures of planes on a paper napkin.

"Why did they crash?" she murmured. "I saw one of them explode. But was it really just one? Or did they collide first?" She closed her eyes to try to visualize the scene, but couldn't do it. "Why else would they have exploded?"

"These air shows themselves are the problem." Wilfried pursed his lips and reached for a bread roll. "Sooner or later, something like this was bound to happen."

Laura shook her head. "There's something else behind this."

Manni lifted his gaze from his jam sandwich. "Why did they crash, then, Daddy?"

"Maybe something broke. Or they were tired. Accidents happen. Just like with driving, only much worse."

"But you always say that only Sunday drivers cause accidents. The Italians aren't Sunday fliers!"

"Nobody knows why, yet," Laura interjected. "But I'm going to find out."

***

Laura drove to the hotel where the Italian squadron was staying.

A casually-dressed man was having a loud discussion with the hotel clerk at the porter's desk. He was very pale, and wore a black mourning symbol on his denim jacket. Fragments of Italian sentences peppered his English; he was obviously having trouble making himself understood.

Laura sauntered up to the kiosk next to the reception. In passing, she heard that the clerk was talking about one of the dead pilots. But once she began flicking through the magazines, she didn't understand any more of the conversation; she was too far away.

Eventually, the clerk left her desk and came back with a chef. The two men had a lengthy conversation in Italian, the gist of which the chef then quietly translated.

Laura went up to the bar and ordered a red wine. She sat at the end of the bar, so that the chef would have to pass her to return to the kitchen. As he approached, she slid rapidly off the bar stool, glass in hand. She bumped into him, and the wine spilled onto her suit.

Laura swore.

The chef stared at her for a moment. "*Scusi, Signora.* Please, come with me to the kitchen. I'll take care of the stain."

She made an effort to look annoyed at first. Then she smiled. "Thank you, let's give it a try." She sighed. "Red wine, of all things!"

"The stain will come out with salt. You'll see."

In the kitchen, she sat down on a folding stool. The chef dug around in a cupboard and pulled out a clean tea towel.

"My name's Laura Schreiner, by the way," she said, as he squatted in front of her. Since he didn't immediately introduce himself, she continued: "I couldn't help seeing how you came to a compatriot's rescue as a translator."

The chef laid the tea towel on his knee. "Actually, the clerk can speak Italian too, but right now..." He looked up quickly, and then spooned salt onto the stain.

Laura was curious as to how he would react to her next words. "The disaster yesterday has hit us all hard."

He nodded. "Why did it have to happen to us, of all people?"

"Yes, why?" Laura echoed. "My little boy says the Italian stunt pilots are better than all the rest." She smiled with motherly pride. "He knows what he's talking about, you know, young as he is."

"Kids are smart; much smarter than their parents." A smile crossed his round face. "I have a little boy too – he's four."

"Mine's nine. But his sister is four. She goes to the Catholic pre-school; maybe she knows your son?"

The chef rubbed the tea towel on the salted stain. "I'm sure she does. I'm Tarcisio, by the way."

Laura took that as a sign that she had gained his trust, and returned to the subject of the pilots. "The guest at reception was wearing a black mourning symbol. Is he a relative of one of the pilots from the crash?"

Tarcisio nodded, brushing the salt from her skirt. "*Sisi*, and he's very angry, because they refused to release any belongings to him. The pilots have been silenced, he says."

"The Mafia taking on the air force? With something like this? I don't believe that," Laura declared.

"Not the Mafia. The Mafia are lightweights compared to them."

She let an instant pass before she asked the next question. "Well, who was it, then?"

The chef stood up and placed the salt shaker next to the stove. He narrowed his eyes as he looked at her again. "Why are you asking all these questions?"

Laura hesitated, and apparently for too long, because the chef frowned.

"Aren't we all interested in it?"

"Why, *Signora?*" The chef came a step closer, looking searchingly at her face.

"You made me curious," she said, evading his question again and smiling.

"You're lying, *Signora*. What are you even doing here, in the hotel?"

She gestured towards her skirt. "You already know that. I wanted a glass of wine."

Tarcisio muttered something unintelligible and slid his hands into the pockets of his apron.

"Go and have one, then. I'm finished. The rest will come out at the cleaner's."

Laura stood up. "I'll bring you the bill this afternoon."

The barman placed a new glass of wine on the counter in front of her with a friendly, "On the house". She drank it, wondering what she should do next.

Then, two men appeared; the older one wore a uniform she didn't recognize. The other wore the bright blue overall that she knew from Manni's photo collection. She looked more closely, and spotted the *Frecce Tricolori* symbol above the officer's badge on his left side. Then she saw the Italian flag on the other man's sleeve as well.

Before long, the clerk passed her and went into the kitchen, returning with the chef. As Tarcisio spoke to the two men, he glanced at Laura several times. Suddenly, she was certain that they were talking about her.

As she was considering what to do next, she noticed that the one in the overall kept looking over at her. She smiled at him. When he returned her gaze, eyebrows raised, she stood up and went over to them. "Can I help you?"

"What are you looking for here? Material for one of your articles?" asked the uniformed man in fluent German.

Laura hesitated in surprise.

"You're not that easy to forget, *Signora*. I saw you arguing with the military police yesterday."

"That was yesterday." Laura looked the younger man in the eyes. "You were staring at me, not the other way around." She turned and left. When she brought the chef the bill from the cleaner's that afternoon, she would ask about the angry Italian hotel guest she had seen at the reception.

***

She drove home, changed and took her skirt to the cleaner's. Then she picked up the children from school and pre-school.

"I think your daughter has an admirer," the pre-school teacher told her. "Luigi's dad asked for your address."

"Who is he, Luigi's dad?"

The woman shrugged. "This was the first time he's picked him up. Normally the grandmother comes."

"Luigi's dad can teach us pizza," Nina piped up. "And spaghetti, of course."

Laura couldn't believe that was a coincidence; it had to be Tarcisio. "Did you talk to Luigi's dad?" she asked her daughter. "Did you make plans?"

Nina shook her head and glanced warily at Manni. "Boys are stupid."

As she drove the children home, Laura wondered why the hotel chef had picked up his son today, of all days.

She dropped them off and knocked at the neighbor's. "Mrs Breiner, I have to go out for half an hour again. Wilfried should be back soon, but would you go and keep an eye on Nina and Manni until then?"

Was Laura imagining it, or did Tarcisio really turn a shade paler when she appeared in front of the hotel kitchen, ten minutes later? "Have you taken an interest in my daughter? The teacher says you've never picked up your son yourself before."

"His *Nonna* is sick," he answered abruptly. "What do you want, *Signora?*"

"I've brought you the cleaning bill."

He took it silently and reached into his pocket for the money, lips pursed. He obviously wasn't planning on talking to her.

At reception, she inquired after the angry Italian civilian, but he wasn't there, and the hotel clerk had finished her shift. Laura was annoyed. She should have spoken to him right away, rather than letting herself get scared off by the two soldiers.

The sirens of an ambulance and two police cars startled her from her thoughts as she drove home. Laura braked as she reached her street to let them pass her. But they turned, and then stopped in front of her building.

Startled, Laura accelerated. She stopped behind the second police car in the middle of the street, and flipped down the sun visor with her press badge. As she ran towards the building, a policeman blocked her way.

She tried to remain friendly. "Let me through, I live here."

"Do you have ID?"

We had enough of this yesterday, she thought, and forced her way past him. Before he could grab her, she ran up the stairs. Voices floated down from above, and then a fireman came down towards her.

"What's happened?" She felt her throat closing.

Two paramedics followed him with a stretcher; behind them came a third, with an IV bag. She looked into Mrs Breiner's battered face. Her blouse was stained with blood.

Laura swallowed; she took the stairs three at a time as she ran on.

Two police officers stood in front of the open door to her apartment. Wilfried was leaning against the wall in the hallway.

Laura took a step towards him. "Where are the kids?" Her voice was suddenly no more than a croak.

"Gone!" A shadow crossed Wilfried's face, and he pulled her into his arms.

"Your children have been kidnapped," said a husky, female voice.

Laura turned around. A young detective that she knew from an interview emerged from the living room.

Wilfried held her tight. "I found Mrs Breiner when I got home."

"And this." The policewoman handed Laura a piece of paper. "Can you tell us what it means?"

Laura took the note with shaking hands. "Keep your hands off, if you want to see the children again."

"Sweetheart, what do they mean?" Wilfried let her go, and cupped his hands around her face.

"What happened to Mrs Breiner?"

"I'm afraid..." He bit his lip and looked searchingly into her eyes. "What have you got yourself into?"

"It sounds like something from a cheap Mafia film, but we should take it seriously," said the policewoman.

Laura remembered the chef's words: not the Mafia. She shook her head. Should she explain her suspicions? "What should we do?" she asked instead.

The policewoman shrugged. "If you can't give us any leads, we can only wait it out."

After the forensic team had finished, they were left alone.

"I'm certain that you know what this means." Wilfried's eyes were narrowed in anger, and for an instant Laura wondered who it was directed at.

She told him about the hotel chef and her conversation with the two Italian officers.

"So it really is the Mafia?" Wilfried's voice sounded sarcastic. "They'll want more than for you to just keep your nose out."

She whispered instinctively. "The Mafia are lightweights compared to them, Tarcisio said this morning."

For several minutes, they sat silently as dusk fell. Eventually, Laura stood up and switched on the light. "I'm going to the hotel. That chef knows something." She clenched her teeth so forcefully that they ground together.

"I'm coming too." Wilfried tugged at his shirt collar and looked at her imploringly.

"What if they call?"

He lowered his gaze. She felt sorry for Wilfried; but she couldn't bear to just sit there and wait, either. She was sure the chef wouldn't talk, but she could at least feel as though she was doing something useful.

✳✳✳

"I've been expecting you, *Signora*," Tarcisio called to her, as she peered through the swinging door of the hotel kitchen's delivery entrance not long after.

The chef cast a look at the two kitchen staff, placed his mincing knife down next to a bunch of parsley and came towards her. He glanced at his hands – they were shaking – wiped them on his apron, and shoved the right one into his pant pocket, while pushing Laura back out into the open with the left.

"We knew you were coming," he whispered.

"Who?" Laura asked, just as quietly. "Tell me."

Tarcisio pulled out an envelope and held it out to her. "I don't know. I don't know anything."

"Of course not." Laura got angry, and snapped at him. "All you know is our address. Who did you give it to?"

He grasped her hand and shoved the letter into it. "Be quiet." Then he walked off, but turned around once more. "You can figure it out for yourself."

She stared after him, until the door stopped swinging. "Just about, yes," she whispered.

As she unfolded the letter in the light of the next street lamp, she shuddered.

"You'll get the children back the day after tomorrow, if we read about the RIGHT reason for the crash."

Goose pimples rose up her legs. "And what is that?" she asked aloud, into the night.

Laura looked at her watch; it seemed decidedly too late to call on hotel guests. But tomorrow, there might be nobody left.

Ten minutes later, Laura was sitting with the Italian in a beer garden, two streets from the hotel. His English was terrible;

her Italian consisted of holiday gibberish. But he had brought a notepad with him, and could draw well. First, he drew the *Frecce Tricolori*: nine airplanes in formation, and one flying towards them; next to that one, "Marco". She understood that this had been the name of the solo pilot.

In the next picture, the solo pilot crashed with one of the planes from the formation, but he immediately crossed this out. *"Impossibile,"* he said. As far as she understood, the pilot would never have remained on a collision course; he had been murdered.

Laura tried, once again, to remember: had the mid-air crash happened before or after the explosion?

"Why?" she asked.

He drew the boot of Italy, then Sicily, and north of that, a row of dots; above one of these, he wrote "Ustica". Next to it, a big airplane nose-diving into the sea, and then "DC 9 – 1980".

Laura knew that one of the islands there was named Ustica. "That plane crashed?" she asked, to make sure. She couldn't remember whether she had read about it at the time. There were so many accidents.

He shook his head and drew a large ship, from which planes were taking off, and another plane that was shooting at the crashing aircraft.

"I don't believe that," Laura let slip in German.

He couldn't have understood her. But he seemed to have correctly grasped either the tone of her voice or her facial expression, because he shook his head again. Then he drew another small plane, next to which he wrote the name of one of the pilots. He also wrote the name of another one of the dead *Frecce* pilots. So according to him, they had both been there, and had seen everything.

Laura chewed her thumbnail and thought for a while. "If

they wanted to eliminate witnesses, why wait until now? This was eight years ago."

He didn't understand her. She wrote '1988' on the sketch with the stunt pilots, and then a question mark. Then she pointed to the date he had written next to Ustica.

He took a deep breath and began again in English. Then he shook his head and switched to Italian. He spoke very slowly: "An appointment; next week, with the judge. They were going to talk."

"And that's why they were murdered now?" Laura narrowed her eyes. She didn't quite believe his story; but Nina and Manni had been kidnapped. There had to be some truth in it. "Who are they? The CIA, or the Italians?"

He finished his drink and stood. "They are dangerous. Why are you asking all this?"

"They have my children."

He stared at her for a second, shocked; then he rested his hands on her shoulders. "*Signora*, the pilots are dead. Other witnesses, too. Do what they want."

He turned and walked away.

***

She had hardly got her key into the lock when Wilfried tore the door open. "My God, where were you for so long? Couldn't you have called me?" His face was pallid, his eyes damp. "Mrs Breiner is dead." He took her in his arms and pulled her into the apartment.

She felt horror, and then guilt, because she hadn't even thought about how worried he must have been. "I was trying to find out who has our kids." Laura sank onto the shoe cabinet and rubbed her burning eyes.

"And?"

"I'm not sure. But I do know what's behind it." She felt deathly tired. "It's a conspiracy." She leaned against him, exhausted. "And now I'm going to be a part of it."

His shoulders tensed under her hands and he breathed in sharply.

Laura closed her eyes before continuing. "I have to spread their lies to get our children back."

Wilfried had his arm around Laura's shoulders as she sat at her typewriter in the morning, and he read along as she typed. "Crash due to pilot error..."

He brushed the tears out of her eyes with his hand: "You can always write a new article."

Laura yanked the paper out of the machine. "They'll always be able to find us."

THE END

If you enjoyed this mini-thriller, please recommend it to others. Reviews and recommendations help other readers to find books worth their while.

If you're interested in information about new releases and free reading material, subscribe to my newsletter:
http://eepurl.com/bHQtvf

About the author:

Annemarie Nikolaus was born in Hesse, Germany, and lived in northern Italy for twenty years. In 2010 she moved to Auvergne, France, with her daughter.

She studied psychology, journalism, politics and history and worked, among other things, as a psychotherapist, an adult-learning teacher, a journalist, a lecturer and a translator.

She began to write literature in early 2001.

Her first printed novel appeared in 2005, a joint work with two other authors called '*Das Feuerpferd*'. Later she has begun publishing independently.

Blog in English: http://bit.ly/2G0ugGJ

If you would like to get in touch:
Patreon: www.patreon.com/AnnemarieNikolaus
Facebook: http://www.facebook.com/AnnemarieNikolaus
Twitter: http://twitter.com/AnneNikolaus

Publications:

In English:

Magical Stories. Short stories for children. Paperback edition ISBN 9782902412600.

Radiant Hope. Illustrated science-fiction story. Paperback edition ISBN 9782902412600.

The Granddaughter. *"Quick, quick, slow - Lietzensee Dance Club".* Paperback edition ISBN 9782493398123

Back onto the Dance Floor. *"Quick, quick, slow - Lietzensee Dance Club".* Paperback edition ISBN 9782493398147.

Falling for a movie star. *"Quick, quick, slow - Lietzensee Dance Club".* Paperback edition ISBN 9782493398130

Broken Rules. Historical crime short stories. Paperback edition ISBN 9782902412686

Silenced. Short thriller. Paperback edition ISBN 9782902412860

Gone... Short Stories. Paperback edition ISBN 9782902412877.

The Piratess. *"Dragon World"* series. Fantasy novel. Paperback edition ISBN 9782902412679

Aquitaine: The End of a War. *"By The Wayside..."* series. Paperback edition ISBN 9782902412808

In German:

Novels and short stories

Historical

Königliche Republik. Historical novel. Paperback edition ISBN 9782902412471

Verjährt. Historical crime short stories. Paperback edition ISBN 9782902412549.

Fantasy

Die Piratin. „*Drachenwelt*" series. Fantasy novel. Paperback edition ISBN 9782902412495

Das Feuerpferd. Fantasy novel, together with Monique Lhoir und Sabine Abel. Paperback edition ISBN 9782902412501

Magische Geschichten. Short stories for children and adults. Paperback edition ISBN 9782902412488

Renntag in Kruschar. „*Drachenwelt*" series. Fantasy anthology. E-Book only

Leuchtende Hoffnung. A Science Fiction novel in Advent calendar form. Paperback edition ISBN 9782902412563

Crime and Suspense

Haus zu verkaufen. Novel. Paperback edition ISBN 9782902412983

Bitterer Wein. »Médoc« series. Mystery. Paperback edition ISBN 782493398017

Ustica. Short story thriller. Paperback edition ISBN 9782902412556. Paperback with voucher for the e-Book.

Tot. Short stories. Paperback edition ISBN 9782902412587.

Verjährt. (see above)

Romance

Die Enkelin. *'Quick, quick, slow - Tanzclub Lietzensee'* series. Love story. Paperback edition ISBN 9782493398093.

Flirt mit einem Star. *'Quick, quick, slow - Tanzclub Lietzensee'* series. Love story. Paperback edition ISBN 9782493398109

Zurück aufs Parkett. *'Quick, quick, slow - Tanzclub Lietzensee'* series. Story of love and marriage. Paperback edition ISBN 9782493398116

Non-fiction

Tourist attractions

Aquitanien: Das Ende eines Krieges. *'Am Rande des Weges ...'* series. Paperback edition ISBN 9782902412570

Background series on literature and books

Suche Reisebegleitung. *Fliegende Blätter.* Paperback edition ISBN 9781499608427

Junge Welten. *Fliegende Blätter.* Paperback edition ISBN 9781500971991